This book belongs to

_____

Published by Advance Publishers
© 1998 Disney Enterprises, Inc.
All rights reserved. Printed in the United States.
No part of this book may be reproduced or copied in any form
without the written permission of the copyright owner.

Written by Ronald Kidd
Illustrated by Arkadia Illustration Ltd.
Produced by Bumpy Slide Books

Based on the book by Dodie Smith published by Viking Press.

ISBN: 1-885222-98-X

10 9 8 7 6 5 4 3 2 1

In a warm, cozy house on the edge of London,
a group of Dalmatian puppies were playing their
favorite game. They called it Cruella De Vil.
"This time I want to be Cruella!" said a pup.

"No, me, me!" cried another.

Off to one side was a shy puppy named Missy. She wanted to play, but as usual didn't quite know how. So she sat by herself and watched.

The puppies decided who would be Cruella De Vil, then dressed for the parts and started to play. First they told the story of how Cruella and her helpers, Horace and Jasper, had kidnapped the puppies. Then they acted out their escape.

They never tired of the game and played it over and over again. Each version of the story was more fantastic than the last.

"I tied Horace and Jasper to the television so everyone could get away," boasted Lucky.

Penny said, "I pulled their hats down so they couldn't see. When they chased after us, they bumped their heads on some tree branches and fell off a cliff!"

"I picked up Cruella with my teeth," Rolly exclaimed. "Then I swung her around my head and sent her flying off into space!"

Missy, wanting to join in the fun, said, "Did I help, too?"

"You just watched, the way you always do," said Freckles. "Anyway, you're too quiet to help. You can't even bark!"

It was true. Missy had never barked — not once in her whole life. "I could if I wanted to," she said in a soft voice.

"Really?" said Freckles. "Then show us."

Missy took a deep breath, threw back her head, and opened her mouth, but it was the same as always. No matter how hard she tried, she couldn't bark.

The puppies burst out laughing, but they were interrupted by a voice from across the room. "That's all right," said the voice. "I can't bark either."

They turned around, and there was Sergeant
Tibs. Several weeks before, Tibs had helped them
escape from Cruella De Vil — in real life, not in a
game. Today he had come to visit the puppies and
their parents, Pongo and Perdita, and their three
pets, Roger Radcliff, Anita Radcliff, and Nanny the
housekeeper.

As the puppies greeted Tibs, Missy studied him thoughtfully. She knew he was brave and kind. But that day there was something else about him that she found a lot more interesting. He was a cat.

Missy had never thought much about cats.
But as she watched Tibs, she started to see what
wonderful animals they were. They were quiet.
They were thoughtful. And they never barked. In
other words, they were just like Missy.

That's when she had her great idea. Maybe she didn't have to be a Dalmatian after all. Maybe she could be a cat!

Missy decided that all she needed was a few lessons, so later that day she went to Tibs for help. When she told him her idea, Tibs looked at her in a funny way. "I say, Missy, do you really think this will work?"

"Just give me a chance," she said. "Please?"

Tibs finally agreed, and Missy gave him a big lick right on the nose. He came away sputtering. "Well, I can see we've got a lot of work to do. The first thing is that cats never lick others. We only lick ourselves."

"That doesn't sound like much fun," she said.

"It's not for fun," Tibs replied. "It's to keep clean."

Missy didn't care much about being clean. She did want to be a cat, though, so she began to lick her paws and legs. She tried to lick her tail, too, but first she had to catch it. She chased it around and around, faster and faster.

Suddenly there was a bump, and Missy went tumbling to the floor. She'd been so busy trying to catch her tail that she'd run into Tibs, knocking him down. "I'm sorry," she said. "I guess I'm not very good at licking."

"Perhaps licking isn't the best way to start," Tibs said. "Let's try something else that cats enjoy: playing with yarn."

Tibs found a ball of yarn and showed Missy how
to hit it back and forth between her paws. But when
she did, the ball began to unwind. Soon there was
yarn wrapped around everything — including Tibs.

"I guess I'm not very good at playing with yarn, either," said Missy sadly.

"Don't worry," Tibs replied. "I know just the thing to try. It's so easy that anyone can do it."

Tibs led Missy to the next room, where Anita was standing by the piano, listening to Roger play.

"Watch this," said Tibs. He glided over to Anita and began rubbing up against her leg. Smiling, she reached down and stroked his back.

Tibs returned to Missy and said, "You see? There's nothing to it."

Missy made her way over to Anita and slowly, carefully, began rubbing against Anita's leg. Nothing happened, so Missy rubbed some more. A moment later she heard someone giggling. It was Anita. "Roger," she said, "look at Missy. She's acting just like Sergeant Tibs."

Roger smiled down at her. "Hey there, Missy, are you turning into a cat?"

Missy was thrilled. Her plan was working!

Roger turned back to the piano and began to sing. Soon he was on his feet, dancing around the room with Anita in his arms. Missy followed along behind, looking for another chance to rub against their legs.

"Psst!" said Sergeant Tibs from the doorway. "Be careful, Missy. Get away from there!"

Missy hardly even noticed him. Besides, what could possibly go wrong? Wasn't she as graceful as a cat?

Just then Roger paused for a moment. It was the opening Missy had been waiting for. She jumped in next to his leg and began to rub.

Everything was perfect, except for one thing:
Roger didn't see her. When he started dancing
again he tripped, grabbed Anita, and the three
of them went down in a heap.

Roger looked up and saw Missy. Scratching her
ears, he said, "You're a sweet dog, Missy, but I
think you'd better go outside for a while."

Roger took Missy into the yard, where Sergeant
Tibs found her a short while later. "It's no use, Tibs,"
she said. "I'll never be a cat."

He smiled sadly. "Sorry, lass. You tried your best."

Missy lay down beneath a tree and sighed. If she wasn't a cat, what was she?

As she stared off into the distance, something caught her eye. Across the street, two men were getting out of a truck, holding big, empty bags. They nodded to each other and silently began sneaking toward the house.

Missy wondered what they could be doing. Then
she saw the sign on the side of their truck. It said
Fur Coats, Inc. The men had come to kidnap the
puppies!

Missy jumped to her feet and raced around to the back door to warn the others. The door was closed, and she couldn't get inside. She tapped at the window, but no one noticed her. Desperate, she looked around for Tibs. He was nowhere in sight.

Meanwhile the men had reached the house and were peering through a side window. What could she possibly do?

As Missy watched the men, she felt a tickle in her stomach. It traveled up to her chest and into her throat, where it changed to a murmur and then to a growl. The growl grew and grew until she couldn't hold it back anymore. It burst from her throat, and before she knew what had happened, she was barking!

"Nice doggie," said one of the men. He
held out his hand, but Missy kept barking. Finally
the man lunged and tried to catch her, but she
scampered away, barking louder than ever.

The door opened, and Roger came outside.
"Missy? Is that you?"

When the men saw Roger, they raced to their truck and drove off down the street. Missy followed them as far as the curb, still barking.

Roger caught up with Missy and gave her a big hug. "I didn't know you could bark," he told her, "but I'm certainly glad that you did!"

Pongo, Perdita, Tibs, and everyone else came running from the house. They gathered around Missy, and she greeted them with a chorus of happy barks.

Missy had saved the day!

Missy is still quiet and thoughtful. But when the other puppies start a game, they always ask her to play. Her brothers and sisters tell Missy she's a hero, but she knows better.

Missy is a Dalmatian, and that's just the way she likes it.

Sometimes I wish that I could be
The puppy in the spotlight —
But for someone shy like me,
It never, ever feels right.
Instead I'll stay just like I am,
And to myself be true.
I'm happy to be me and hope
You're happy being you!